Saginaw Chippewa Academy LMC
JFIC FIC HUG
Hughes, Moni Jan's big bang /
92200
P9-CBF-308

WITHDRAWN

Monica Hughes

Jan's Big Bang

Illustrations by Carlos Friere

FIRST NOVELS

The New Series

Formac Publishing Limited
Halifax, Nova Scotia

Formac Publishing Company Limited acknowledges the support of The Canada Council and the Nova Scotia Department of Education and Culture in the development of writing and publishing in Canada.

Canadian Cataloguing in Publication Data

Hughes, Monica, 1925-

Jan's big bang

(First novel series)

ISBN 0-88780-384-9 (pbk) ISBN 0-88780-385-7 (bound)

I. Freire, Carlos, 1943– II. Title. III. Series.

PS8565.U34J36 1997 jC813'.54 C96-950223-0
PZ7.H87364Ja 1997

Formac Publishing Limited
5502 Atlantic Street
Halifax, NS B3H 1G4

Printed and bound in Canada.

Table of Contents

1
Jan's Great Idea

Going to a new school is kind of scary. "And how long have I got to share a room with you?" I ask Mom when we move in.

"Just as long as we're staying with Gran. Once Dad's found a job it'll be different. Be thankful we've got a place to stay."

I *am* thankful, really. Especially now that I've got a best friend, Sarah. We do all kinds of fun stuff together. Like the Science Fair. There are signs all over the school:

SCIENCE FAIR COMING
MAY 18TH

"I don't see why *we* can't do something. Let's ask Mrs. Nelson."

"You mean you and me? She'll say our grade's too young, I bet. And what'd we do anyway?"

"In my last school some of the kids made a model of a volcano from mushed-up paper and glue, painted to look like grass and rocks. They filled the hole inside the volcano with baking soda."

"That's weird," says Sarah. "Why'd they do that?"

"Well, they coloured vinegar red and poured it in the hole and it all came burping out the top and running down the sides, all red and foamy. Like a *real* volcano."

"Great. Let's do it." Sarah grins.

Then the bell goes and we have to run.

Just before recess I put up my hand. "Please, Mrs. Nelson, may *we* be part of the Science Fair?"

"You?" Mrs. Nelson looks surprised.

"Me and Sarah."

"Grade Threes don't usually…"

"*Please*."

"Well, why not? There's an easy book on projects in the school library. I don't think it'll be too hard for you to read. But ask me if you need any help."

"We won't, thank you," Sarah says. We look at each other and we're both thinking: *Just wait till the kids see our volcano.*

"Anyone else want to try?" Mrs. Nelson looks at the rest of the class, but no one says anything. You can tell by their faces they think we're crazy. For just a second I wonder if we *are.* But then I think: *Ours will be the only Grade Three project in the whole fair. Great!*

The bell goes and we all head out of the classroom.

"Just don't try the baking-soda-and-vinegar volcano," Mrs. Nelson calls after us. "After the mess last year the principal said, 'Never again.'"

"Oh-oh, we've got a problem," Sarah mutters.

"Now what'll we do?" I stop in the middle of the hall.

"There's that book in the school library," she suggests.

2
No Problem!

During lunch break we find the book on science projects. It's got lots of pictures and not too many words.

"This sounds good. 'How to build an ant farm.' Do you like bugs?"

"If they don't have too many legs. I can't *bear* centipedes." Sarah shudders. "But ants are okay. Let's go for it."

There's a picture in the book with all the things we need for this project. "A mason jar with a screw ring. A little bottle to fit inside."

Sarah leans over my shoulder. "What's this? Oh, a square of nylon from pantyhose. And a sheet of black paper. And dirt."

"Any special kind, do you suppose?" I ask. We read what the book says. Just ordinary garden dirt.

"Something's missing," Sarah says.

"What?" I stare at the picture.

"The ants." She giggles.

"Very funny. Getting ants'll be easy. We've got zillions and zillions in our lawn."

"I can get paper and one of Mom's old nylons. Is a mason jar the same as a jam jar?" Sarah frowns at the picture in the book.

"No, it's a sealer, with a screw-on ring. Gran has a pantry full of pickles. Cucumber pickles and beet pickles. The beet ones are *disgusting.* Their juice is like purple blood."

"Ugh! So can you get a jar?"

"No problem. The empty pickle jars are in the basement."

"That's okay. Then we need a moist sponge and some food. That's easy."

We make a list of everything, and after school Sarah goes home and gets the nylon and some construction paper, and I get a small jam jar out of the recycle bin and a mason jar from the basement. We meet out in the yard and start work on our great project.

There's no problem putting the small jar upside down in the mason jar and then filling the space around with dirt. I borrow a couple of Gran's tablespoons and it works great. Then we have to catch the ants.

We break the top off one of the ant hills. They come boiling up into the grass and run around very fast. They look kind of mad and it's hard to catch them without squashing them.

"Ow, they're running up my arm!" Sarah yells. She jumps up and starts brushing herself. "Yuck!"

"I thought you liked ants," I tease.

"Not tickling me all over, I don't. Jan, this isn't going to work. I've only got one in the jar so far and he doesn't look too good."

"If only we could *tempt* them in." It sounds dumb, but I can't

think of anything else.

Sarah looks at me like I've just come up with a great invention.

"Wow, you've got it!" she says.

"I *have*?"

"Sure. Think of picnics."

I think of picnics. "Okay."

"And ants."

I look down at the ants running madly round in the grass and then I do get it. I remember trying to eat a peach on a picnic. Practically all the bugs in the world wanted their share.

I take the spoons into the kitchen. I wash off the dirt and smear a bit of honey on them. Not too much. We don't want their feet to stick as we shake them into the jar.

Gran comes in just as I'm licking my fingers. "If you want bread and honey just ask, Jan. But dipping your finger in the jar is disgusting."

"Sorry, Gran." I run outside with the spoons.

We put the spoons flat against the ground and wait. The ants come running. It's like they sent out a signal to all their friends. COME AND GET IT!

All we have to do is shake the ants off into the jar and lay the spoons down again for the next lot to climb aboard. In no time at all we've got plenty.

One of the things the library book said was to put in some ant babies. They're called 'larvae' and they look like cottony grains of rice. We dig down with the spoons and get a bunch of them and scatter them over the dirt in the jar. At once all the ants begin picking them up and carrying them around in their mouths.

"It's working already," Sarah says, breathing down my neck as I hold up the jar. "They're turning into a family."

"Food," I remember. "And drink. Here, you take the jar. Make sure they don't get out."

I run into the bedroom Mom and I share. There's a collection of tiny sponges she uses for putting on her makeup. I borrow one of them and wet it under the bathroom tap. Then I stop in the kitchen.

"Gran, please can Sarah and I have some cookies?"

"Sure, honeybunch. But I've

only got store-bought. Oreos or chocolate chip?"

I think about it. "Can we have both?"

I take out the plate of cookies and the sponge.

"Hurry," Sarah says. "Some of them want out."

"They won't when they see what we've got for them." I drop the damp sponge on top of the dirt and put the plate down in the grass. "Which kind do you think they'll like best?"

"Chocolate chip," says Sarah.

"Hmm. I like Oreos better," I argue. So we put in bits of each and eat the rest.

Sarah fastens the piece of old nylon pantyhose over the top of the mason jar. "Great," I say. "We've done it. Easy."

"But I only have purple paper to wrap around the jar," Sarah says. "I guess the black got all used up last Halloween."

"I bet the ants won't know the difference," I tell her.

We tape a sheet of purple paper all around the jar so the ants will be in the dark and think they're underground. Then I put the jar on one of the shelves in the pantry.

"There you are, little ants. Hurry up and build a city. We'll leave you in peace."

Our Science Fair project is ready to go. No problem.

3
Surprise for Gran

Next day, Sarah's big brother John bikes by us on the way to school. "Silly Sarah says you've got a science project for the fair."

"So?" I say to him.

"Bet it won't work," he says and rides on.

"Never mind *him*," Sarah says. "He's always like that."

The bell rings and we go into class.

"How's your project going?" Mrs. Nelson asks.

"Just great," we say together.

All we have to do is make sure that our ants don't run out of cookies or water.

"What are you doing?" the other kids ask.

Sarah and I look at each other. "It's a secret," we say together and start giggling.

"All right, girls. Settle down," says Mrs. Nelson.

I dream about our ants making tunnels and rooms and looking after their babies.

After school we go to the mall for an ice cream to celebrate our science project.

"Say hi to the ants from me," Sarah says as we go home.

I go into the living room to talk to Mom. She's got her feet up and she's reading the paper. Suddenly there's a crash and the horrid sound of breaking glass. Gran screams.

Mom and I run into the kitchen. Gran's holding an empty cylinder of purple paper in her hand. There's dirt and broken glass all over the floor, and the ants are busy running around trying to pick up their babies.

"What in the world ...?" Mom gasps.

"Our ant farm. Gran, you broke our ant farm!"

"The jar just slipped out of my hand. I thought it was beet pickles. Oh, my, it gave me a start!"

"You sit right down, Mom," says my mom to Gran. "As for you, Jan..." Boy, is she mad.

"I'll help clean it up." I run for the broom.

"You'll stay out of harm's way till I get rid of this broken glass."

I hand her the broom without a word and go back to where Gran is sitting, fanning herself.

"I'm sorry, Gran," I whisper. "I didn't think ..."

Mom hears my whisper. "You didn't, did you?" she snaps. She empties the dirt and glass into a garbage bag. "What on earth were you doing with ants in Gran's pantry?"

"It was a Science Fair project. For school."

Mom's usually keen on school stuff. It doesn't work this time. "You clean every last ant out of this kitchen," she says. "I don't want to see a single one. And don't you ever bring insects into this house again. Okay?"

I've never seen Mom so mad. She puts her arm around Gran

and hugs her. "Are you all right, Mom?" she asks my Gran.

Gran pushes her glasses up onto her nose and gets up. "Of course I am. Don't be hard on the child. It was just a little surprising, that's all."

I do love my Gran.

4
Now We've Got a Problem

"We've got a problem." I tell Sarah about it on the way to school next morning.

"Oh, dear. John didn't believe we had a real project. If we give up now he'll never stop teasing."

"Who said anything about giving up, Sarah? We'll think of something."

"Maybe something else in that library book?" she suggests.

"No good. It's all insect projects. Mom says no more insects." The bell goes. "How's your project coming?" asks Mrs. Nelson as we go into class.

Sarah and I look at each other. "We had a small accident," Sarah says at last. "But don't worry. We'll be ready for the fair."

On the way home we stop at the mall for an ice cream to cheer ourselves up.

There is an exhibit on recycling at the mall. There's a bin for composting garden waste and kitchen scraps. Beside it there's a smaller box, with a crowd around it.

"What is it?" Sarah asks.

"I can't see."

"It's a worm composter," the woman standing in front of me says. "It's partly filled with dirt and torn up newsprint. And worms, of course. You feed them your kitchen scraps."

"Why?" I ask her.

"The worms turn the garbage into beautiful garden dirt. They've got leaflets explaining, if you want to…"

But we're not listening any more. Sarah and I look at each other. Our problem is solved.

"Are you thinking what I'm thinking?" she asks.

"You bet. Let's go!"

We run off.

"It's so easy. Just digging up a bunch of worms," Sarah says.

"And I've got a plastic tote box with my winter sweaters in it. It's got a really tight fitting lid. We can use that. I'll stuff the sweaters in the back of the closet."

"Where will we keep it? My house is no good. John's too nosy."

"I only promised Mom I wouldn't bring insects into the house. Worms aren't insects, Sarah," I remind her. "We'll hide the box behind the sofa in the basement, so Gran won't open it by mistake. This project is *really* going to work!"

5
Worms to the Rescue

The new science project is going really well. We dig up some lovely fat worms and they're in my sweater box, munching away. Every day Sarah and I add some kitchen waste.

After we've been feeding the worms for three or four days we begin to get worried.

"Phew, it smells!" Sarah holds her nose.

"Perhaps we've been overfeeding them. Let's leave them in peace for a few days."

So we do. On Wednesday Sarah has a birthday party.

On Friday morning Gran says, "Be careful if you go down to the basement. The light at the top of the stairs has gone and I don't have any more bulbs till I go shopping tomorrow."

I imagine the worms munching away in the dark, turning garbage into compost for Gran's tomato bed. Neat!

Sarah's brother John rides his bike around us as we walk to school.

"Quit that," says Sarah.

"How's the famous science project going, Jan?" he asks.

"Just dandy," I tell him.

"Really?" He wiggles his eyebrows up and down in a sneery sort of way and rides off.

"He's such a creep," Sarah sighs. "You're lucky not having a

brother."

"I guess so." John is a tease, but sometimes I get a bit lonely, being an only child. An older brother might be kind of nice.

"Believe me," Sarah says firmly.

"How is your project coming along?" Mrs. Nelson asks again as we go into the Grade Three classroom.

"Just fine," we tell her. I wish she wouldn't keep asking. It makes me nervous. I think about the worms munching away. I cross my fingers and hope.

6
Basement Spooks

The Science Fair is on Monday. On Saturday morning, Sarah comes over to my house. She has sheets of white cardboard from the packets her mom's pantyhose come in. And a box of felt pens. We are going to write the sign for our project.

"We ought to have 'before' and 'after' signs," she says.

"If we have a 'before' sign, there should be something to show. Like maybe some fresh food scraps," I remind her.

"Great! We can collect scraps from Monday's breakfast, so

they won't be icky. Only there's nothing left at *our* house after breakfast. Mom says John eats like a vacuum cleaner."

"I'll bring the breakfast left-overs. Toast and the skin off a banana..." I check off on my fingers. "And a tea bag."

We sit at the kitchen table and make the signs.

SCRAPS THAT END UP IN LANDFILLS, Sarah prints on one piece of card.

SCRAPS THAT TURN INTO COMPOST TO HELP THE GARDEN GROW, I print on the other.

"We should have our names on them," Sarah reminds me.

We write 'Sarah Smith' and 'Jan Macleod' and 'Grade Three,'

so everyone will know it's our project.

"That looks great!" Mom whirls into the kitchen, sips a cup of instant coffee, and takes a bite out of a bagel. "Whoops, I'm late." She puts down her cup and half a bagel and heads for the door.

It is very peaceful when she's gone. Gran is out getting groceries. We have the house to ourselves.

"Let's just check on our worms," Sarah suggests. "Maybe they've finished all the scraps and are starving for more."

We open the basement door and I click on the light. Nothing but darkness. I remember what Gran said.

"Darn. The bulb's gone."

"Do you have a flashlight?"

"No battery," I tell her. "But Gran keeps a candle and matches in case of a thunderstorm."

The candle is on a shelf in the pantry. I light it and we go carefully downstairs.

How different everything looks! Shadows dance around the room. The washer and dryer are like scary Halloween coffins. The furnace ducts are like the arms of an octopus stretching out across the room. Gran's old dressmaker dummy seems to jump at us like a headless monster.

Sarah stands so close to me I can feel her shiver. "Hurry up," she whispers. "It's spooky down here."

"The tote box is right behind the sofa." I try to keep my voice steady.

The lid fits really tightly.

"You take the candle, Sarah," I tell her, and then I pull off the lid.

7
There's Got to be a Way

BANG!

There is a flash of greeny-blue light and then darkness.

Sarah drops the candle. We both scream.

"Find the candle quick," she yells.

I grope around the floor. "Here it is. Where are the matches?"

As we grope for the matches, I smell the most horrible smell. Like...like *very* rotten vegetables. Sarah finds the little folder and strikes a match and lights the candle.

We peer into the tote box.

"Pee-ew!"

There is no crumbly brown compost. There are no lively worms. My sweater box is filled with a wet icky mess.

There goes our science project, I think, in deep despair.

We hear Gran's feet in the kitchen overhead, putting away the groceries. She opens the basement door and screws a new bulb into the socket at the top of the stairs. The light comes on and we blink at its brightness. I blow out the candle.

"What are you children doing down there? And *what* is that awful smell?"

We both try to explain about the worm composter and the greeny-blue flash and the bang.

"I can't make heads or tails of this," Gran says. "Come upstairs and explain it to me one at a time and slowly. I'll make us some lemonade."

After we've told her exactly what happened we show her our beautiful signs.

"What a shame!" she says. "You didn't know that you were supposed to buy special worms to make compost?"

"Special worms?" Sarah and I look at each other.

"I guess we should have taken a leaflet from the display in the mall," Sarah says.

"What made it explode, Gran?"

"Methane gas," Gran explains. "Sometimes called marsh gas. It comes from rotting garbage. It can be a problem in landfills. Explosive. As you found out. Which reminds me, please get that smelly mess out of my clean basement!"

We put the lid on the tote box and take it into the yard. Life is truly depressing.

When Sarah says, "John will tease us to death," I feel like crying.

No, Jan, I tell myself. *There's got to be a way out of this problem.*

I give a big sigh and say, "Let's see if we can find a really quick science project in the city library."

"Nothing with insects or worms," Sarah reminds me.

We go to the library and look for 'Science Projects' in the junior encyclopedia. Most of them are very difficult. Some of them take a long time.

"Here's one about the atmosphere," Sarah says. "It just takes two empty pop bottles with their tops covered with balloons."

"What for?" I lean over her shoulder.

She reads aloud: "Set one bottle in a pan of hot water and the other in a pan of ice cubes. The balloon over the bottle sitting in hot water will fill up with air from the bottle. The other will remain empty. This shows that air expands with heat."

I sigh. "Very boring, but the fair *is* on Monday."

Sarah says slowly, "Air's a kind of gas, isn't it?"

"I guess so."

"So's methane," she says, and I get it.

"Sarah, you've saved our project! All we need to do is to write new signs."

8
It's a Bomb!

On Monday we set up our display in the gym. We have a large pop bottle half filled with rotting garbage. We have another large bottle half filled with fresh breakfast scraps. Each of them has a balloon tightly fastened over the top.

The balloon over the garbage bottle is already puffed up after sitting right through Saturday and Sunday. The balloon over the other bottle hangs limply down.

In front of our display is a big sign:

METHANE GAS IS
PRODUCED BY
ROTTING GARBAGE.
WARNING: EXPLOSIVE!!!

At the bottom of the sign are our names and the words "Grade Three."

Mrs Nelson walks by. "How original!" She beams.

The principal walks by. "Grade Three! My goodness. I suppose Mrs. Nelson helped you?"

"No, we thought of it all by ourselves," we tell her.

Sarah's brother John says, "Hmm. Not bad." Sarah's smile goes from ear to ear.

Everyone looks at our display. It's great. We feel like rock singers or hockey stars.

Then the principal makes a short speech. She introduces a

Very Distinguished and Important Visitor from the School Board. He makes a long speech.

"Boring," whispers Sarah.

"Sshh," I whisper back. "Scientists have to learn patience."

The Very Distinguished and Important Visitor stops talking. He looks at the displays. We wait patiently, like good scientists, until he stops at our display.

" 'Methane gas is produced by rotting garbage,' " he reads aloud. "That's bad, isn't it?"

We nod.

"So what should we do with our garbage?"

"Compost it," we manage to gasp.

He smiles. "Good for you." He looks at the display again. " 'Warning: Explosive,' " he reads.

"How do you know it is?"
"Because it did," we tell him.
"Really? This I must see for myself," he says. He takes out a cigarette lighter.
"Oh, no!" I yell.
"Don't!" yells Sarah.
But the Very Distinguished and Important Visitor isn't listening. He flicks on his lighter and flips the balloon off the pop bottle.
BANG!!
"What was that?" someone shouts.
"It's a bomb. Everyone outside!" shouts someone else.
"It's only garbage," I try to explain. No one is listening.
"It's just *gas*!" Sarah shouts.
"GAS!!" Someone hears her and rings the fire alarm.

9
Being a Scientist is Fun

After the fire drill we all go back to our classrooms. Everyone agrees that it is the most interesting Science Fair the school has ever had.

Mrs. Nelson runs her hands through her hair. She only does this when she is frantic.

"To think I stopped you two from demonstrating how a volcano works. Oh, my!"

"Our project certainly went with a bang, didn't it, Mrs. Nelson?" I say to cheer her up.

Being a scientist is fun. I look at Sarah.

"So what'll we do next year?" she asks.

Meet five other great kids in the New First Novels Series:

- **Meet Morgan the Magician**
  in *Morgan Makes Magic*
  by Ted Staunton/Illustrated by Bill Slavin
  When he's in a tight spot, Morgan tells stories — and most of them stretch the truth, to say the least. But when he tells kids at his new school he can do magic tricks, he really gets in trouble — most of all with the dreaded Aldeen Hummel!

- **Meet Duff the Daring**
  in *Duff the Giant Killer*
  by Budge Wilson/Illustrated by Kim LaFave
  Getting over the chicken pox can be boring, but Duff and Simon find a great way to enjoy themselves — acting out one of their favourite stories, *Jack the Giant Killer*, in the park. In fact, they do it so well the police get into the act.

- **Meet Robyn the Dreamer**
  in *Shoot for the Moon, Robyn*
  by Hazel Hutchins/ Illustrated by Yvonne Cathcart
  When the teacher asks her to sing for the class, Robyn knows it's her chance to be

the world's best singer. Should she perform like Celine Dion, or do *My Bonnie Lies Over the Ocean*, or the matchmaker song? It's hard to decide, even for the world's best singer — and the three boys who throw spitballs don't make it any easier.

- **Meet Carrie the Courageous in** ***Go For It, Carrie***

by Lesley Choyce/ Illustrated by Mark Thurman

More than anything else, Carrie wants to roller-blade. Her big brother and his friend just laugh at her. But Carrie knows she can do it if she just keeps trying. As her friend Gregory tells her, "You can do it, Carrie. Go for it!"

- **Meet Lilly the Bossy in** ***Lilly to the Rescue***

by Brenda Bellingham/ Illustrated by Kathy Kaulbach

Bossy-boots! That's what kids at school start calling Lilly when she gives a lot of advice that's not wanted. Lilly can't help telling people what to do — but how can she keep any of her friends if she always knows better?

Look for these First Novels!

- ***About Arthur***
  Arthur Throws a Tantrum
  Arthur's Dad
  Arthur's Problem Puppy

- ***About Fred***
  Fred and the Stinky Cheese
  Fred's Dream Cat

- ***About the Loonies***
  Loonie Summer
  The Loonies Arrive

- ***About Maddie***
  Maddie in Hospital
  Maddie Goes to Paris
  Maddie in Danger
  Maddie in Goal
  Maddie Wants Music
  That's Enough Maddie!

- ***About Mikey***
  Good For You, Mikey Mite!
  Mikey Mite Goes to School
  Mikey Mite's Big Problem

- ***About Mooch***
  Mooch Forever
  Hang On, Mooch!
  Mooch Gets Jealous
  Mooch and Me

- ***About the Swank Twins***
  The Swank Prank
  Swank Talk

- ***About Max***
  Max the Superhero

Formac Publishing Company Limited
5502 Atlantic Street, Halifax, Nova Scotia B3H 1G4
Orders: 1-800-565-1975 Fax: (902) 425-0166